CHRISTMAS

COLORING BOOK FOR KIDS AGE 4-8

Over 40 Snow Globe Coloring Book Pages For All Children, Girls and Boys

Merry Christmas

MERRY CHRISTMAS

MERRY CHRISTMAS

MERRY CHRISTMAS

MERRY CHRISTMAS

MERRY CHRISTMAS

Printed in the USA
CPSIA information can be obtained
at www.ICGtesting.com
LVHW072312251223
767374LV00013B/318